I0760735

A Timmy Dennison Story

by Tom Beaudin

Bladensburg, Maryland

Published by
Inscript Books
a division of Dove Christian Publishers
P.O. Box 611
Bladensburg, MD 20710-0611
www.dovechristianpublishers.com

ISBN: 978-1-957497-66-2

Printed in the United States of America

To faithful Christian counselors,
working to preserve God's plan
for spiritual, physical, and psychological wellness.

Preface

It has been a little more than three years since the publication of Ya Gotta Outmaneuver 'Em. During those years, people have asked me if I would be writing another book. My answer has always been a simple, "I don't know." You see, I don't consider myself to be much of a writer, at least not one with a compulsion to publish for the sake of publishing; were that the case, I'd be a starving wannabe. Neither do I think I'm much of a storyteller; I pretty much live in the moment, void of fictional creativity.

Looking back, I suspect that Timmy's Spiritual Christmas originated in the heart of an educator seeking to explain to youngsters, through simple storytelling, some perhaps controversial theological concepts. I received little reaction (neither positive nor negative) from the youth; however, I did get considerable reaction from adults. *Go figure.*

Of course, there is a plethora of scriptural topics to be explored for the youth (and, as it turns out, for some adults as well). Is there such a thing as a miracle? Do angels exist? Do they dwell among us? Why does God let bad things happen? Does free will exist, or does God orchestrate everything? What is God's timing? How does one really forgive? The list is endless, and while I don't pretend to be a theologian, there are often some simple explanations that will, at least temporarily, satisfy the inquisitive young mind.

In addition to some of the aforementioned common theological issues, there is an abundance of "growing up" situations faced daily by maturing youths. One can look at these situations through a variety of lenses.

It is no surprise that the world is broken, but it has been broken for quite some time. Since the disobedience of Adam and Eve, what was created as a perfect world has been less than perfect. History will show that civilizations have come and gone, marked by periods of growth and success but followed by periods of social and moral deterioration. The pendulum stops swinging only when the decline becomes irreversible.

Many believe that the United States is currently in moral and social decline. Attempts at re-writing history abound; long-admired statues are being torn down; raging mobs disrupt social order; blind justice is on the wane as select groups seek to overthrow the justice system; moral decline is evident as church attendance is on the wane; the nuclear family has been decimated by single parent households, a variety of sexual aberrations, and challenges to biblical values; our education systems are in free fall; and the country is split 50/50 on good and evil with each side accusing the other of being the evil one. The trouble is that good and evil have left the realm of objectivity for a more subjective determination. Will the proverbial pendulum continue to swing, or has the nation reached a point of irreversible decline?

The answer, I believe, lies in scripture. Proverbs 23:18 says, "There is surely a future hope for you and your hope will not be cut off." Romans 12:12 picks up on that thought and expands it, saying, "Be joyful in your hope, patient in affliction, faithful in prayer." Yes, we live in an imperfect world, but it's not void of conquering hope and love.

Young Timmy Dennison is a lucky young man. He faces all the imperfections of a damaged world, but he does so wrapped in the bubble of hope and love from a family and church guided by scriptural beliefs and values. Timmy's story is never meant to show him as the "model child" in the "model family," always doing right and never doing wrong. Rather, it is meant to show, quite simply, that God's way is the better way and will see him through life's trials and tribulations.

Psalm 27:1,2

"The Lord is my light and my salvation - whom shall I fear? The Lord is the stronghold of my life - of whom shall I be afraid?"

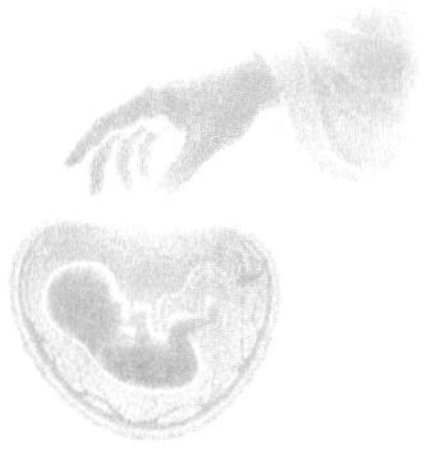

Prologue

Timmy Dennison sat glued to his seat as the Master of Ceremonies called on Mr. Bennett, the girls' soccer coach, to present the awards to members of the girls' soccer team. It was the Fall Sports Assembly at Wynhope High School, and members of all the fall sports teams, along with their parents and friends, were in attendance.

Mr. Bennett had coached the relatively inexperienced girls' soccer team to a respectable 7 - 4 win/loss record. With a team of six starting freshmen, his young team had done surprisingly well on the season, and there was little doubt that the future held promise for a league and possibly state championship.

One by one, he introduced the girls, offering a brief comment about each. Finally, he turned to the table where several trophies were lined up. The anticipation in the room was electric.

Timmy was in attendance supporting his friend of several years, Jessica Billings.

Jessica, or Jess as she was called, was a natural athlete. Her baseball skills were already legendary (in Little League and middle school), and, as an incoming freshman, she had yet to bless the high school softball team with her talents. Although she hadn't played soccer until this year, there had been little doubt that she would do well; she did not disappoint.

Mr. Bennett picked up the first trophy and began, "Our first award tonight goes to the most improved player. Last year, as a sophomore, she saw limited playing time. However, she attended a three-week summer soccer camp a few months ago and has shown tremendous improvement in her skills and ability to read the field. I'm proud to present this trophy to Missy Erlich."

Missy came forward, was handed her trophy, and received hugs and handshakes from those on the dais.

"The next award," continued Mr. Bennett, "goes to the defensive player of the year. There is no doubt that several of our wins came because of our goalie, Becky Wilson, who, game after game, shot after shot, seemed to have eyes in the back and sides of her head and the quickness of a hunter cat. Becky, come on up and receive your well-deserved trophy."

Becky walked to the dais amidst the cheers of

teammates and parents, received her accolades, and returned to her seat. The anticipation increased as the two remaining trophies screamed for an owner.

Mr. Bennett once again grabbed the mic. "Of course, with a defensive player of the year, it can only follow that we should have an award for the offensive player of the year. This choice was literally a no-brainer for our coaches. With statistics of fifteen goals and eleven assists to corroborate the obvious, coupled with the irony of name-position, the selection of our striker, Selena Stryker, was a lock. I'm happy to present our best offensive player award to Selena.

Selena walked to the stage, urged on by the raucous cheers of teammates, friends, and family. Humility could have been Selena's middle name. The cheers of fans during a game never bothered her, but this kind of recognition, where all eyes were suddenly on her, embarrassed her. She'd rather run ten laps around the field than walk the few steps to Coach's outstretched hand. Graciously, she thanked Coach for his praise, received her trophy, and returned to her seat.

All eyes were now focused on Coach Bennett as he slowly stepped once again to the mic, holding the last trophy. After a long moment of hesitation that bordered on indecision, Mr. Bennett began. "Our last award is really two awards combined into one. A 'best overall team player' is the one who plays a variety of positions, who knows the game like the back of her hand, and who has given her best effort to be an exceptional teammate. An 'MVP' is a player who might not be the best overall but who still brings a lot to the table with team support, team spirit, and reliability both on and off the field. Our last award combines all the attributes of both those categories. This year, we are calling it the 'Most Valuable Teammate' award. I should note that this is a unique award in that it was voted on by members of the team. In near unanimity, the Wynhope High School girls' soccer team has chosen as their most valuable teammate, Kylie Winslow."

Kylie was a new student who had transferred to Wynhope from a school in the adjoining state. She hadn't made many friends but was popular with her teammates, who immediately embraced her unassuming ways. Her skill set had been evident from her first appearance at practice. As she approached the podium, those in the audience who had followed the team for the season stood and applauded. Her teammates high-fived and clapped her on the back as she walked by them. Slowly but deliberately, she made her way to the podium. Coach Bennett cited several highlights of her play throughout the season and then graciously thanked her for her contribution to a surprisingly successful season.

When Coach Bennett handed her the trophy,

Kylie paused as if unsure of what to do next. Then, rather than returning to her seat, she slowly turned and walked toward the left end of the stage, where Mrs. Pilsner, the principal, and Mr. Hogan, the athletic director, were sitting. Timmy looked in obvious surprise at his friend Jessica but got no discernible reaction. Without a word, Kylie placed her trophy at Mr. Hogan's feet, and instead of returning to her seat, she ran from the room. The silence in the room was deafening. People were flabbergasted. Looks of dismay and surprise prevailed. No one knew what had just happened.

No one, that is, except Timmy…

James 1:19

"My dear brothers, take note of this: Everyone should be quick to listen, slow to speak, and slow to become angry,..."

Chapter One

Two weeks before the first day of school

"Ladies and Gentlemen," began the Chair, "welcome to our special Board of Education meeting, called this evening in order to allow the citizens of Wynhope the opportunity to share opinions and data regarding the Board's proposal to remove three books from our elementary school curriculum. I refer specifically to the second-grade book, '*God Created Her/Him*,' and the two fifth-grade books, '*There's a Boy Inside Me*,' and '*My Body - My Decision*.'"

So began what many had hoped would be the end of several weeks of phone calls, emails, and texts that had interrupted the anticipation of a new school year. Wynhope, a small rural conservative town, was not unlike other surrounding small towns—faced with an influx of people who were deserting the "woke" practices of the larger urban areas, but who ironically were bringing with them many of those same practices and beliefs that they were fleeing. There was an obvious sense that the Wynhope citizenry was unhappy with some of the liberal trends and was attempting to restore the small community atmosphere that had once been an earmark of the town.

The three books in question had become a huge controversy in Wynhope. While many defended making the books available in the library, few were in favor of including them in the curriculum. The whole issue was symptomatic of a growing distrust in an administration dealing with a vocal minority of residents who were demanding diversity, equity, and inclusion. Fresh in the minds of many were the unreasonable mandates imposed during the COVID-19 crisis. The anger of many was directly proportional to the exposure of the fraud that was gradually surfacing in the media. In short, "politics" was rapidly becoming a factor in the education of Wynhope's youth. Parents, feeling the loss of control over what their children were being taught and exposed to, were adamant about regaining control of prior conservative values.

Joshua Dennison, a history teacher at the Wynhope Middle School, and his wife, Brenda, were in attendance at the meeting. The Dennison family was a long-time resident of Wynhope. Josh and Brenda had three children, two of whom, Lindy and Matt, had already graduated from high school and were attending college. Their youngest, Timmy, had just begun his freshman year at Wynhope High. As members of The Way, a Christian church, they were particularly glad to see so many of their church family in attendance on this evening. Also in attendance was their pastor, Rev. Stephen Remy.

More than two dozen staff members from the three schools were also in attendance. That they seemed to be segregated into two distinct groups lent credence to the fact that there was an obvious conservative/liberal split among the educators. Fifth-grade teacher Sheila Hines, who had been disciplined the previous year for her classroom decor and activities during Pride Month celebrations, vocally defended the inclusion of the three books in the curriculum. Equally expressive was the newly appointed school resource officer, Edwin Bailey, a conservative.

To their credit, those assembled managed to calmly and factually state opinions and suggest solutions, minus the finger-pointing and name-calling that often characterized these types of meetings. Finally, two and a half hours into the meeting, the Chair once again took the mic and addressed the crowd. "I am beginning to hear some arguments for a second and even third time; several people have spoken more than once. So, I believe that it is time to close this meeting, return to our homes, and ponder the many excellent points that have been made this evening. I thank you for your attendance this evening and assure you that the ideas and thoughts expressed here tonight will be thoroughly considered by the Board of Education. Our next regularly scheduled meeting will be three weeks from tonight, when, barring any unforeseen circumstance, the Board will make its decision. I will now entertain a motion to adjourn."

The motion was made, seconded, and the meeting was adjourned. Slowly, little groups of like-minded people gathered informally, spoke together for a few minutes, and then made their way to the parking lot. Josh and Brenda Dennison spoke with Pastor Remy and a few other people from The Way before climbing in their car and heading home.

Hebrews 13:6

"So we say with confidence, 'The Lord is my helper; I will not be afraid. What can man do to me?'"

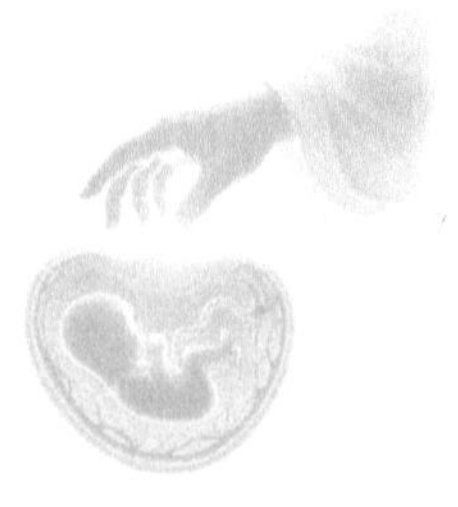

Chapter Two

Two months before Fall Sports Assembly

"Hey, Jess, wait up." Timmy quickly jogged down the sidewalk in front of the school to catch up with his friend, Jessica Billings. Girls' soccer practice had just ended, and after spending an hour and a half in the library working on his homework, Timmy had waited patiently for Jess on the front steps of the school. Somehow, she had slipped by him and was walking around to the north side of the school and the gym entrance, where she presumed he might be waiting.

Although it was the first day of classes at Wynhope High, soccer tryouts and subsequent practices had already entered their third week. Jessica—Jess to her friends—was known for her baseball/softball prowess, but, in fact, she was an all-around natural athlete. So, since there was no fall softball, it was a no-brainer for her to try her hand (or foot) at soccer.

Timmy had befriended Jessica and her twin brother, Jeff, a few years before when they had moved to Wynhope, and in the ensuing years, he and Jess had become best friends. This was in no small way due to Timmy's fanatical interest in baseball and Jess's natural talent as a switch-hitter. She had become the "talk of the town" after her first Little League tryout. By the end of her Little League career, she held every record ever recorded in the Wynhope Little League. As a middle schooler, she had transferred her extraordinary skills to the school's softball team, and as an entering freshman, she was looking forward to what seemed to be a far-too-distant spring season.

"Haven't had a chance to catch up with you since classes started," Timmy said breathlessly. Timmy lived only a couple of blocks from Jess, and they often walked the mile trip to and from school together. There wasn't much that they didn't discuss and share with each other. "How are your classes lookin'?" he asked.

"Old man Bayer for Algebra," Jess replied. "That guy never cracks a smile. Miss Aldrich for English; I think this is her first year teaching. All the guys think she's really hot. Burnett for Social Studies, Alvarez for Spanish, and good ole 'Father Nature' for Science." Because of his summer job at a local camp where he often took the young campers on nature walks, Mr. Ryan had earned his very popular nickname, "Father Nature."

"No homework tonight, so, right now, I'm liking them all," Jess said. "What about you?"

Timmy, who took all the same subjects except for French instead of Spanish, launched into a lengthy discourse about his teachers, two of whom were friends with his dad because earlier in their careers, they had taught at the middle school where his dad was a teacher. In addition, the Dennison name was no anomaly at Wynhope High. Timmy's brother, Matt, who had graduated a few years earlier, had the same French teacher that Timmy now had. Timmy also had a sister, Lindy, but she was seven years older, so he didn't remember much from her high school days. Changing the subject, Timmy offered, "That new girl who transferred to our school is in my English class; her name is Kylie Something-or-other. I overheard her saying that she had moved from another state and..."

"Kylie Winslow," interrupted Jess. "She only moved to town a few weeks ago, so she missed all the pre-season stuff, but she showed up at practice today and asked Coach Bennett if there was any possibility she might get a chance to play. She explained that she had played on her middle school team before she moved. Coach said, 'Sure,' so she sat right down on the bench, changed into her soccer shoes, and joined in the drills for the rest of the afternoon.

Now you know, I'm not much of a soccer buff,

but this girl's got talent; she's fast, a great passer, and looks to be a great two-footed player. After practice, she didn't hang around; she just changed into her daytime kicks and headed back into the building.

"Coach called us together after we had finished our laps, gave us a run-down on tomorrow's game, and before sending us to the locker room, he gave us a heads-up on Kylie."

Thirty minutes earlier:

"I know that some of you have met Kylie in your classes," Coach began, "but I wanted to give you all a little bit of background so that you might welcome her to the team. Mr. Hogan, the Athletic Director, alerted me this morning that she might show up at practice. Apparently, he knew the details of her transfer and had spoken with her middle school coach. He indicated that she's a pretty talented player but that she has a rare skin disorder that prompted her family to move to the Wynhope area in order to be closer to her medical specialist. Obviously, she is sensitive about the issue, so she'll wear pantyhose to cover the blemishes. Mr. Hogan has orchestrated a few exceptions that he hopes will accommodate her medical concerns and secure her privacy. She'll most likely use the nurse's facility rather than the locker room for practices and home games. Mr. Hogan is working

on arrangements for away games. I'm sure that you guys'll welcome her and help her to settle in here at Wynhope."

Jess continued. "I almost bumped into her as she was leaving the nurse's office. We chatted for a few minutes - talked about some of the kids on the team, her class schedule, and all that stuff. She seems really nice. I told her that if there was anything she needed as she was getting settled, that you or I would be glad to help out. Hope you don't mind me offering your help."

Timmy seized Jess's pause in her story. "Actually," he began, "she was pretty talkative when Mrs. Kingston did her opening day exercise of each student introducing themselves and sharing with the class. She talked about her move to Wynhope in order to be closer to her doctor, although she didn't mention anything about her disorder. What I really liked was how she described her close relationship with her grandmother, 'Nana.' You know how I feel about my 'Gram' and what an important part of my life she has been."

Timmy's Gram (his maternal grandmother) lived just a few doors from his family. In his younger years, when Mom and Dad were working and Matt and Lindy were always busy at school, Timmy spent almost every afternoon with Gram and Gramp, his grandfather. They nurtured him, they taught him, and they "loved him to death." When Gramp died a few years back, Timmy was devastated, but with time, he recovered and became very protective of Gram, often doing chores around her house and keeping her company whenever he could. As school became more demanding and his schedule more complicated, Timmy struggled to find time for his Gram—but she always remained his top priority..

As they neared their usual point of separation, Timmy said, "Hey, Jess. How about you stop with me and spend a few minutes with Gram? Heck, ever since I introduced you two, she always asks me how you're doing. She's become your biggest baseball fan."

"I'd love to stop, but I promised Jeff that I'd help him with painting his room. Oh man, I can taste those chocolate chip cookies from here. How about a raincheck?"

"You got it. See you in the morning."

"Later…"

Hebrews 4:15

"For we do not have a high priest who is unable to sympathize with our weaknesses, but we have one who has been tempted in every way, just as we are - yet was without sin."

Chapter Three

Teachers, as well as students, will tell you that some of the toughest days of the school year are the first few and the last few. Excitement, the unknown, and the chaos that result from both tend to disrupt the normal flow of the school day. The next few weeks flew by as the school settled into the mundane flow of normalcy.

Well into the third week of school, the Board of Education held its regular monthly meeting. The second item on the agenda was "A Resolution Regarding Three Elementary School Books." Since this item had been previously opened to public discussion in a special meeting, discussion was restricted to Board members only. The Chair allowed each Board member to relate anything that they felt might be important to the decision. When all had spoken, the Chair said, "I will now entertain a motion regarding the books."

Immediately, Mrs. Hall moved "...that all three books be removed from the curricula and from the school's libraries." The motion was seconded, and after a brief discussion, it was defeated 6 - 3, largely by those who were principally opposed to book bans. Not ready to concede her position, Mrs. Hall made a second motion, this one to "remove the books from the curricula but to allow them to reside in the libraries for use 'with parental consent.'" Quickly, the motion was seconded. Having largely expressed their opinions on the first motion, discussion was minimal, and the motion passed 7-1 with one abstention.

The next three items on the Board's agenda were policy revisions that had been prepared and read at the previous regular meeting. These were approved with no discussion.

As was the Board's policy, the final agenda item was "public comment." This had been instituted in years past to allow any taxpayer to bring a concern before the Board. It was understood that this was an opportunity to present an item that the Board would consider and act on in the future. Since there was a larger-than-usual attendance at this particular Board meeting, the Chair suspected that this might be due to either the book issue or something that had been previously discussed among select groups of taxpayers.

The first to comment was Mr. Dryden. "My name is Luke Dryden," he began, "and my wife and I are the proud parents of Samantha, an eighth grader at the middle school. Many parents, and even some educators, are not aware that Congress has designated September 17 of each year as 'Constitution Day.' In addition, September 17 - 23 of each year is 'Constitution Week.' In 2004, Public Law 108-447, Section III was passed; it requires the following:

"'*Each educational institution that receives Federal funds for a fiscal year shall hold an educational program on the United States Constitution on September 17 of such year for the students served by the educational institution.'*

"Now, I don't know what Wynhope School System did this year to fulfill its legal obligation, but I do know that at least one staff member took the mandate seriously, and I wish to congratulate and applaud Samantha's history teacher, Mr. Dennison. Samantha shared with me the materials that Mr. Dennison had prepared and discussed with his classes. In these times when criticisms abound, I think that it's appropriate to recognize Mr. Dennison for his patriotic attention to law."

The chairman responded. "The Chair thanks you, Mr. Dryden, for your recognition of Mr. Dennison and notes your subtle reminder of observing Constitution Day. Are there any other comments?"

Surrounded by her own cadre of supporters, Mrs. Cochran rose to be recognized. When called on, she stumbled a bit before securing her verbal footing and began. "My name is Sharon Cochran. My husband and I are long-time residents of Wynhope; our two children have attended Wynhope schools since like forever. Currently, they both attend the high school. Last week, my daughter's best friend had to see her guidance counselor in order to make a schedule change that would enable her to have Band in her schedule. Upon entering the counselor's office, she immediately noticed a poster on the bulletin board that was obviously printed and distributed by Planned Parenthood. As I recall, the Board has already adopted policies on sexuality, sexual orientation, abortion, and other gender issues; essentially, it has said that these were topics for the home and not for school. That this counselor, whom I will not name in a public meeting, would provide information by or for Planned Parenthood is unconscionable." When she finished and sat down, her supporters applauded.

"Thank you, Mrs. Cochran. As you know, issues involving staff are serious in nature. I assure you that Mrs. Pilsner will collect information on your concern and that the Board will, as soon as possible, take action in executive session. I should note here that members of this Board are very cognizant of societal changes, and while there are some things over which we still maintain control, State and Federal guidelines must be adhered to. Are there any more public comments?" He looked around the room. "Yes, sir; please stand and state your name."

An older gentleman slowly stood, gingerly balancing himself with his cane. "Good evening. My name is Joel Lawson. I'm a long-time resident of Wynhope. As you probably have guessed, I don't have children in the Wynhope school system." There were chuckles all around. "The last time I attended a school was probably longer ago than most of you are old." More chuckles. "I don't remember too much from those days so many years ago…" Taking off his hat, he pointed to a scar on his balding head. "I think this here scar from a shrapnel wound in 'Nam musta lost me some brain power." Still more chuckles. "Anyway, what I do remember is that we would begin each school day by standing, facing the American flag displayed in the classroom, and reciting the Pledge of Allegiance. I'm here tonight to ask the Board to consider two things: first I would like to see the Board of Education meetings begin with a recitation of the Pledge; second, I would like the Board to consider a policy requiring a properly displayed United States flag in each classroom, and requiring that each student have the *opportunity* to publicly recite the Pledge at the beginning of each school day. Thank you."

There was a pregnant silence before the Chair spoke. "First, Mr. Lawson, on behalf of the School

Board, and I will presume the town of Wynhope, let me thank you for your service to our country. I assure you that your requests will be among our future considerations." Pausing for a moment, he continued, "Are there any other comments for this evening?" Pause. "Seeing no hands, I will entertain a motion to adjourn."

"So moved."

"Second."

"Anyone opposed? Meeting adjourned."

Psalm 16:1

“Keep me safe, O God, for in You I take refuge.”

Chapter Four

Ten years before

As *Nana* put the final few stitches in the red and white dress, she turned and called to the kitchen, "Kylie, sweetheart, come on into the sewing room; I've just finished a new dress and want you to try it on to see how it fits."

Moments later, Kylie appeared in the sewing room. Dressed in a yellow sun dress, hair having earlier been put into a French braid, four-year-old Kylie obediently removed the yellow dress and put the new one on for Nana to make the final fitting. "O, Nana, I love it; can I wear it later when we go to the carnival?"

For more than a year, Nana's grandchild, Kylie, had been living solely at Nana's house. Kylie's mom was currently in a residential recovery facility that specialized in alcohol addiction. Sadly, Kylie's dad had committed suicide the day Kylie was born. Nana had been awarded temporary custody when Kylie's mom was committed to the rehab house.

On most days, Nana would visit with her friend, Miss Betsy. Sometimes Miss Betsy came to Nana's house, and sometimes Nana and Kylie went to Miss Betsy's home. Miss Betsy (also known as Betsy Hogan) was a widow whose son and daughter lived in another state, where her son was a teacher. She seldom saw either of her children, and as a result, she had built a life around socializing with other women her age.

Of course, Nana, Miss Betsy, and their friends all fussed over Kylie. Several of them had knitted scarves, mittens, and hats for Kylie. On this particular day, Nana and Kylie were going to meet up with some of Nana's friends and enjoy the afternoon at the carnival in town. Kylie loved going to the carnival. It was a happy time because of all the fun games, exciting rides, and delicious food. Dressed in the new red and white dress that Nana had made, Kylie knew everyone would make her feel like she was "queen of the carnival."

When they arrived at the parking area next to the carnival, Kylie sensed the excitement in the air. Once out of the car, she held tightly to Nana's hand as she took in the sights and smells of the carnival. She literally tugged on Nana's hand as they hastened to the gate. Once inside the gate, they paused as Nana reminded Kylie where the bathrooms were and that she should only go there with her or with Miss Betsy.

After they roamed the grounds for a while, Kylie asked, "Nana, can we go to see the horses?" Of course, she was referring to the carousel with its colorfully painted horses and lively organ music. They walked to the carousel, where they stopped and took in the sights of glimmering lights and painted horses. After a few minutes, Kylie pointed to a golden steed with a red saddle and proclaimed, "That one, Nana." Nana helped her into the saddle and stood nearby holding on to the brass pole. Slowly, the carousel began to turn, and Kylie squealed with delight.

Later in the day, tuckered out from the day's activities, they found a park bench. They sat with Miss Betsy, all three sharing a warm bag of popcorn and some cotton candy while basking in the warmth of a day filled with fond memories.

On the way home, Kylie asked, "Nana, when Mom gets better and comes home, do you think we can bring her to the carnival and show her all the fun, exciting things?"

"Of course, Honey. Let's plan on it."

Proverbs 3:5,6

“Trust in the Lord with all your heart and lean not on your own understanding; in all your ways acknowledge Him, and He will make straight your paths.”

Chapter Five

Early in October, Timmy had a day with no homework and decided to watch the girls' soccer practice while waiting for Jess. A few minutes into the practice, Coach Bennett realized that he had left his previously determined outline for the day's drills in Mr. Hogan's office. He had stopped there earlier in the day to clear some game schedule changes necessitated by drainage problems caused by recent heavy rains. "Hey Timmy," he beckoned. "Can you come here for a minute?" Timmy hustled over, and Coach asked, "Can you do me a big favor? I left my clipboard on Mr. Hogan's desk. Would you run up to his office and grab it for me?"

"Sure," said Timmy and hustled off to the athletic wing. For some unknown reason, the door was locked. Timmy banged and banged on the door, hoping that anyone inside might hear and open the door. Apparently, there was no one around, so he jogged all the way around to the main entrance of the building, easily entered the building, and made his way all the way back to the athletic wing. Mr. Hogan's office appeared empty, so Timmy knocked on the door. When there was no answer, he tried the doorknob and, to his surprise, found it open. He entered and walked over to Mr. Hogan's desk. The first thing he saw was a letter on the upper right corner of Mr. Hogan's desk from Mr. Bennett announcing his resignation as girls' soccer coach, effective at the close of the season. This surprised Timmy because Mr. Bennett had coached girls' soccer for several years. In the middle of the desk was Coach Bennett's clipboard. Timmy grabbed the clipboard and started to leave when, out of the corner of his eye, he noticed the folder that had been beneath the clipboard. In big red letters, it was marked, "*Confidential.*"

Timmy stared at the folder for a long moment, trying to resolve the instant internal conflict between his curiosity and his years of moral training. He knew exactly what he wanted to do, and he knew exactly what he should not do. Dilemma over, wrong choice won out! He opened the folder, figuring, "*I'll just take a quick peek.*" It was a good thing that no one was around. Almost instantly, the blood drained from his face, and he instinctively looked around to make sure that no one was looking. As often happens, one bad choice begets another, and as he ran from the room, he unconsciously exclaimed, "HO-LY S---"

A few minutes later, having somewhat recovered from his shock, he handed the clipboard to Coach Bennett and ran over to Jess, who was in the middle of doing wind sprints. "I gotta go," he exclaimed. "Meet me at Gram's."

Surprised by her friend's sudden change of plans, Jess said a brief "OK" and watched as he turned and ran toward home.

Timmy took a slight detour on the way home and stopped at the cemetery where his once best friend and confidant, Gramp, had been laid to rest a few years before. Timmy still believed that Gramp's spirit was present with him; because of that, he seldom visited the cemetery; he just didn't feel the need. Today was different; somehow, he was drawn to the gravesite where he could speak out loud to Gramp without worrying about being heard.

He made a beeline for the gravesite, and before reaching it, he blurted out, "Gramp, I just screwed up—big time. You taught me so much, right up 'til you went home to be with God. But you're not here now, and I'm stuck; I sure could use your help. I know that you'd know exactly what to do and that you'd give me the best advice. But you're not here now, and right now, Gramp, I don't know what to do next. Should I tell Mom & Dad? Should I tell Jess?

Should I risk even telling Kylie? You always taught me that God knows, understands, and forgives, but His understanding doesn't fix my mistake. How stupid can I be? I never shudda looked at that folder. Sure wish you were here to give me some advice. Well, maybe Gram will come up with some ideas." Somewhat relieved that he'd gotten part of the heavy load off his chest, he headed to Gram's.

Twenty minutes later, Timmy was breathlessly running up Gram's driveway. Ever since he was little, he had never knocked on Gram's and Gramp's door. It seemed that it was a given that one of them would always be home just waiting for him to come bursting through the door. As if he were still six or seven, he burst through the door into the kitchen. "Gram, where are you?" he shouted.

"Cool your jets, young man," said Gram as she entered the kitchen from her sewing room. "What, pray tell, has you all fired up?"

Timmy caught his breath. "Gram," he said without looking at her, "I just stopped to talk to Gramp. I know that probably sounds funny, but I need his advice. In my heart, I know that he's already given me all the wisdom that God would let him give me, but I'm so shook up that it just all escapes me. Anyway, I'm in deep stuff. I just did a major no-no, and now I don't know what to do."

In her own gentle way, Gram calmly said, "OK,

let's sit, cool down, and you can tell me all about it. Do you want a snack first? I made some oatmeal-raisin cookies this morning."

"That mighta worked when I was little, Gram, but food isn't gonna help me now." With that, he began to tell her what had transpired earlier in the afternoon. When he got to the part of opening the confidential folder, he shamefully looked away, and just as he was about to continue, he was interrupted by a knock on the door. He figured that it was Jess and, relieved for the brief break, he jumped up to let her in."

"Well, hello, young lady. It's been quite some time," welcomed Gram.

Jess gave Gram a big hug. After all, Timmy's Gram was her Gram. Turning to Timmy, she inquired, "So what the heck's going on?"

"You heard Coach ask me to go get his clipboard, didn't you?" he began. "Well, it took me a while 'cause the gym door was locked and I had to go all around...Anyway, I found the clipboard, and as I was leaving, I noticed a file that had been under the clipboard; it was marked 'confidential.' Naturally, that got my interest up. I hesitated, because I knew that the file was private and certainly none of my business..."

As if on cue, Jess's cell phone rang, and she answered it. Timmy and Gram watched as she listened silently, the color seemingly draining from her face. "OK, Mom," she finally said. "I'll be home as fast as I can." Turning to Timmy, she said, "I gotta go; my little brother, Josh, fell off his bike and apparently broke his arm. Mom took him to the ER and wants me home pronto."

She started out the door when Gram said, "Let me drive you home, Jess. It'll be much faster." Turning to Timmy, she said, "We'll talk more later. Lock the door for me when you leave to go home."

***

Timmy had hoped to leave Gram's with the heavy burden of his 'secret' off his chest, but on this occasion, her unceasing love and spiritual wisdom would have to wait. Left with no alternative, he locked up for Gram and headed home.

Timmy's mother and father had raised their children to always tell the truth. At the age of fourteen, Timmy knew in his heart that no matter what, truth was the way to unburden his feelings of guilt. But he also figured that the upcoming confession and discussion probably weren't appropriate for the dinner table. As he was helping with the dishes after dinner was done, he finally got things going by saying, "I've got something important that I need to discuss with you guys ..."

Before he could finish, Mom interrupted. "Timmy, dear. It doesn't take a rocket scientist to see that you've had something on your mind. Your silence during dinner has been deafening. Your Dad and I are happy that you still feel the need to come to us with your joys and concerns, and we're always available whenever you want."

A bit later, Mom, Dad, and Timmy settled in for their discussion. Timmy related the events of the afternoon, ending with his breach of integrity. "I knew it was wrong," he said, "but the temptation to know what was confidential for Mr. Hogan was just too great. The bad part is that I wish I had never found out what I found out."

"Before you consider telling us what that is," began Dad, "you have to weigh whether or not it's too confidential for Mom and me to know. Should you think that, then your problem and any possible solution belong only to you. We wouldn't be able to be of much help. On the other hand, if you feel it necessary to confide in us, perhaps, with God's help, we can find a path of resolution."

"I think you need to know," said Timmy, and then he blurted out, "Kylie, the girl who transferred to Wynhope this year and plays on the girls' soccer team, isn't a Kylie … she's a Kyle."

There was a moment of silence while Timmy's statement settled in. Finally, Mom asked, "Timmy, are you sure?"

"Mom, you haven't raised the village idiot. I know what I saw. I know what was written there."

"Well," started Mom, "my first thought right now is for this poor kid in a new town, in a new school, and without family or friends. Who's to help her bear her obvious and tremendous burden?"

Dad stepped in. "Your Mom is exactly right, Timmy. Whatever you decide as you move forward, I'd hope that your first move would be to consider how you might help Kylie relieve her burden. Jesus showed time and again how His concern and absolute love for all people prompted Him to embrace those who were hurting and feeling rejected. You, and maybe Jess and other classmates, are being called to show godly love to Kylie, whether or not you all agree with her choices. I suspect that a genuine expression of love and concern will, more than anything else, give Kylie some needed support, and maybe even help her begin to make changes in her life."

Dad continued. "Right about now, I'm guessing that you would like this whole situation to disappear off the face of the earth. Unfortunately, that ship has sailed, and so now, as you move forward—as we all move forward—a loving attitude will not only help Kylie and others, but it will be the best medicine to restore your own sense of well-being."

Their discussion continued for the better part of half an hour. When pretty much everything had been said, Dad suggested that they pray and seek counsel from the Lord. He led them in prayer, asking for God's wisdom and truth. Timmy asked for relief from the burden he was carrying, and Mom sought God's protection for Kylie, God's precious creation. She prayed that neither Kylie nor her guardians would fall victim to the gender dysphoria claims of healing through chemical and/or surgical transitioning techniques.

The calming effect of affirming their faith and trust in God's intervention allowed for a sense of peace that enabled a night of peaceful sleep and a start to a whole new day.

At breakfast the next morning, silence prevailed. It was as if no one wanted to address the proverbial "elephant in the room." Finally, Dad broke the silence. "I have some thoughts and ideas on how we might proceed; since this involves all of us, I'd like to run them by you before we make our first move. First and foremost, our situation stems from a breach in confidentiality; it's absolutely critical that, however we proceed, we've got to protect the privacy and confidentiality of everyone involved. Timmy, that comment is directly aimed at you; you know how rumors spread like wildfire; you've got to keep this under your hat at least through the initial stages. That includes your friend and confidant, Jess. Can we agree to that?"

Reluctantly, Timmy nodded in the affirmative.

"Next," he continued, "I am going to leave early for school this morning with hopes that I will get an opportunity to meet with Mrs. Pilsner, the principal, and alert her to a problem she may or may not know about. If she knows about Kylie, there's a huge problem for the school and the Board of Education; if she doesn't know about Kylie, there's a huge problem of a slightly different kind for the school and the Board of Education. In short, while we may have a grave concern for the health and well-being of Kylie, the school and Board of Education will have to deal with the fact that they have had a boy playing on the girls' soccer team all season long."

"I'd have to say that I'm on the same page," said Mom. "Timmy?"

"OK."

Timmy left for school at the usual time and met up with Jess at their usual meeting spot. Her first words were, "Sorry I had to bug out so fast yesterday. Thanks to your Gram, I made it home just in time to be there when Josh and Mom got home from the hospital. I was the first to sign his cast!" Pausing for a moment, she continued. "So, you never got to finish your story yesterday. You got as far as the confidential folder when we were interrupted."

Timmy had figured that this was coming and had already examined his possibilities. He reasoned that he could tell Jess the truth (which he promised Dad he wouldn't do) or he could lie and risk losing a friendship down the road. Until he opened his mouth to answer her, he had no idea what he would do. *Tell her the **other** truth,* came the thought out of nowhere. *The other truth?* O yeah, in all the excitement, Timmy had totally forgotten about Coach Bennett's resignation. "When I went to get Coach's clipboard yesterday," he began, "I saw a letter on Mr. Hogan's desk. Looks like Coach Bennett is resigning as girls soccer coach at the end of this season."

Jess looked at him quizzically. "So?"

"Well, Gram has a friend in her Bible study class whose son is looking for a job," Timmy weakly responded. Wanting desperately to change the subject, Timmy hesitantly suggested, "You know, I've watched a lot of practices; it doesn't seem like that new girl, Kylie, is very close to anyone. Whaddya think about asking her to sit with us at lunch?"

"That won't be an easy task. In our times together on the field, she is friendly but in a sort of standoffish way. She sure doesn't seem ready to embrace a 'bestie.'"

"Won't know unless we try. You with me?"

"I'm in. I'll try to catch up with her at practice today."

When they arrived at school, Timmy immediately noticed that Dad's car was parked near the front entrance. Having been distracted by his usual trek to school with Jess, the sudden realization of what might be going on this very moment in Mrs. Pilsner's office was a gut punch that set the tone of discomfort and anxiety for Timmy's school day.

1 John 5:14

"This is the confidence we have in approaching God: that if we ask anything according to His will, He hears us."

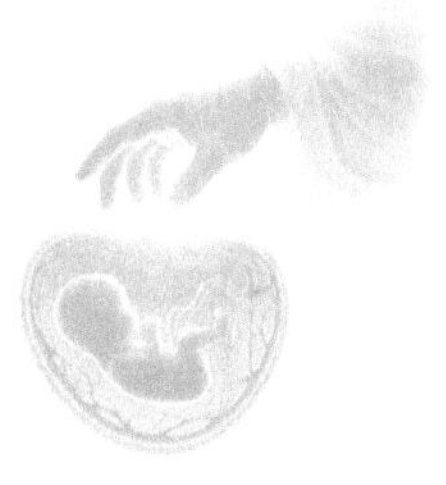

Chapter Six

Inside her closed-door office, Mrs. Pilsner listened attentively to Timmy's dad, who relayed the story as he knew it. When he finished, she reached for her phone, dialed her secretary, and said, "Judy, would you please find someone to cover Mr. Hogan's first-period PE class and then call him and ask him to please come to the office."

Mr. Hogan received the request rather matter-of-factly; it was not unusual for him to be called to the office. Frequently, in his position as Athletic Director, he would have to address an interscholastic issue that just couldn't wait.

When he got to the office, he knocked on the door and entered when invited to do so.

"Cliff, this is Josh Dennison," Mrs. Pilsner said. "Josh teaches history at the middle school and has a son, Timmy, who is a freshman here. Josh, this is Cliff Hogan, our Athletic director."

The two men acknowledged each other before Mrs. Pilsner continued. "Cliff, through an unfortunate, or maybe fortunate, series of events, which I will address with other people at a later time, I now believe that a student, one Kylie Winslow, who entered our school this year as a freshman transfer and who has played the entire season on the girls soccer team, is, in fact, a boy. I also believe that you are, and have been, fully aware of this student's gender status. Josh Dennison is here because it is he, through information that his son confided in him, who, just this morning, has made me aware of Kylie's status. My role here is not to make judgments on gender dysphoria and/or people who opt for gender transitioning. My role as principal of this school is to abide by the laws of the State, the rules of the Board of Education, and the jurisdiction of our interscholastic conference. This meeting is simply to inform you and Josh that I will devote all my energies to a thorough investigation in the next few days. While I have no way to enforce an order of silence, I would strongly recommend that you both maintain a high degree of privacy. I will be speaking with you both individually in the days to come. Please return to your classes now." So began a few days of intense fact-finding, soul searching, and problem-solving.

As soon as the two men left the office, Mrs. Pilsner once again picked up the phone and dialed her secretary. "Judy, would you please drop what you're doing, find out where Kylie Winslow is, and then escort her to my office."

When Kylie entered the office, Mrs. Winslow invited her to relax and sit. "Kylie," she began, "first let me assure you that there is no emergency at your home and that you're not here because you're in trouble." Kylie exhaled and smiled. Mrs. Pilsner continued. "This morning, I was made aware of your gender status. I will assume that your silence regarding that status indicates a lot of family and personal decision-making that you have chosen to keep private. I want to assure you that I will do everything I can to preserve your privacy."

Kylie responded with a relieved, "Thank you."

"However," Mrs. Pilsner continued, "there are issues that must be addressed, and I want you to be a part of any resolutions. First, though, it's important that we include your parents in our discussions."

"That's gonna be kinda hard," responded Kylie. "My dad is deceased, my mom is committed to an alcohol rehab facility, and my temporary guardian, Nana, my mom's mom, lives miles away in my former town of residence."

Visibly shocked to hear all this, Mrs. Pilsner asked, "With whom do you live? I mean, who's on record to contact regarding school communications?"

"I live with Mr. and Mrs. Adolph Bartram on Spencer Road in Wynhope."

"So, what is your connection with the Bartrams?" queried Mrs. Pilsner.

There was a long pause before Kylie answered. "Mr. and Mrs. Bartram have no children of their own. Mrs. Bartram is the daughter of Nana's best friend, Betsy Hogan. She's also the sister of Mr. Hogan, our athletic director."

Had that information been dynamite, the explosion would have been heard for miles around. Instead, there was a pregnant silence while Mrs. Pilsner regained her composure. Finally, she broke the silence. "Kylie," she began, "let me repeat that you are not in any trouble. That being said, I am going to inform Mr. Hogan and Coach Bennett that you will be ineligible to play in the remaining girls' soccer games. Our Interscholastic Committee has definitely ruled that boys are ineligible to play on girls' teams. For your own protection and privacy, I am granting you permission to be absent for the next few days while we address the issues facing us. If you should choose to stay home, I'll make arrangements with your teachers so that you won't fall behind in your schoolwork."

"Thank you, Mrs. Pilsner. I need some time to think this whole thing through and maybe seek out some advice."

Kylie left to return to class. Coincidentally, the bell had rung, ending the first period, and the hallways were in the usual in-between chaos. Kylie headed to her locker, picked up her English class books, and made her way through the throngs to class. Confused and concentrating on nothing but everything, she bumped into someone at the classroom door. "Timmy Dennison," she loudly reacted. "Watch the hell where you're going, will ya?"

More shocked than Kylie was, Timmy mumbled, "Sorry." Then he looked up, realized who it was he had crashed into, and said, "Oh, um, Kylie. Sorry. My head was somewhere in never-never land. Are you OK?" Not waiting for an answer, he impulsively continued. "Hey! I need to talk to you. Any chance we can meet up at lunch?"

"Whaddya want?" asked a disturbed Kylie.

"It's important. But not here."

"OK. I'll look for ya at lunch."

1 John 1:9

"If we confess our sins, He is
faithful and just and will
forgive us our sins and purify
us from all unrighteousness."

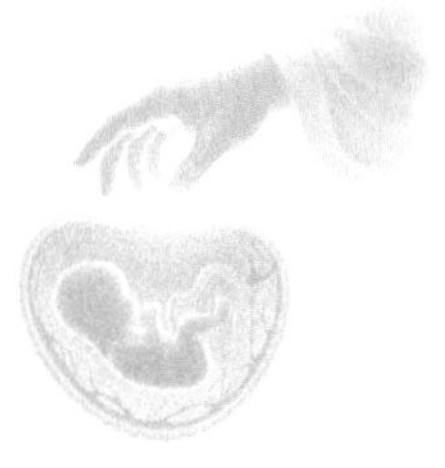

Chapter Seven

Lunch came and went. Timmy scanned the lunchroom every few minutes, but Kylie never showed. Later in the day, as had become his practice, Timmy spent an hour or so in the school library working on his homework before heading to the soccer field to watch the final minutes of Jess's practice. On this day, with a lot on his mind, he contemplated leaving early and going to visit Gram, where problems always seemed to be relieved and his cluttered confusion cleared. Instead, he sat on the bench near the school's front door and lost himself, going over and over the recent events. He was startled to see Kylie walking out the front door; he was even more startled when she walked over and sat next to him. "Is practice over already?" he asked.

"I *couldn't* go to practice today."

"Tough one to miss with tomorrow being the last game," said Timmy.

Ignoring his retort, she said, "I've got a little time before my ride shows up. What did you want to talk to me about?"

Timmy had been ready for this at lunchtime; now, he was caught off guard and sort of unprepared. "I owe you an apology," he blurted out.

"What? For almost taking me out before English class?"

"No. Something else. I'm aware that you're going through a little bit of hell right about now, and I need to tell you that I'm responsible. I'm the one who read a confidential file and talked about it with my parents. My Dad, then, felt it necessary to alert Mrs. Pilsner. In short, I know that you used to be a boy."

"Technically, I still am," was Kylie's response. "I only just started hormone therapy a few months ago."

With that, a half-hour discussion followed during which Timmy offered some of the details that had occurred in the last couple of days. For her part, Kylie told of her connection to Mr. Hogan and how she had come to transfer to Wynhope High. She was open and honest, perhaps even relieved to unburden herself of the heavy secret that she had been carrying. She even expressed some doubts that she was on the right path. With the wisdom of Solomon, Timmy seized on her ambivalence and offered, "I don't know how to help you, Kylie; I wish I did. Nobody should go through alone what you've described. All I can say at this point is that I'm ready and willing to stand with you as a friend. I consider myself one lucky dude. I grew up having one problem after another solved by talking with my Gram and Gramp, along with my Mom and Dad. In all those years, they relied on their unwavering faith in a loving God. Don't know where you are with religion, but I do know that my friend and pastor, Stephen Remy, would be more than happy to spend time with you and help you sort things out."

"Thanks, Timmy. I appreciate your telling me everything; especially, I appreciate your offer of friendship and help. I'm no dummy; I knew from the get-go that sooner or later, truth would prevail. In spite of the recent changes, I'm kinda relieved to maybe look at a different perspective. In the past few years, I've seen a bunch of school counselors and other 'professionals' who seem to agree that a sex change will stop this constant feeling I have that I'm in the wrong body. When my current doctor told me that only a gender transition would solve my discomfort, I started with the female hormones; so far, I don't feel any better; in fact, if I'm being honest, I feel worse. I'm starting to think that I'm just plain crazy. Right about now, I'm open to anything. I am taking a few days off from school with permission from Mrs. Pilsner, so I've got nothing but empty time. Do you think you could make the connection for me?"

"Absolutely. How do I get in touch with you?"

Just then, Kylie's Uber pulled up. She and Timmy quickly exchanged phone numbers, and she said, "I haven't given this out to anyone, so please, no one else."

"Got it," responded Timmy. "No one else. I'll get back to you."

While Kylie was getting into her Uber ride, Jess came walking around the side of the building from the gym entrance. "Was that Kylie I just saw you talking to? She totally blew off practice today, so I didn't get a chance to talk with her."

"Let's head for home," began Timmy. Remembering Dad's words about keeping confidentiality, at least through the initial stages, Timmy weighed in his mind whether or not the 'initial stages' had gone by before continuing. "Jess, as you know, my Gram and Gramp have been more than just grandparents to me. They've been my confessors, my advocates, my advisors, and my best friends for as long as I can remember. When Gramp died, I was devastated. I still sometimes talk to him as if he were right here next to me." He paused.

"What's that got to do with you talking to Kylie?

"Nothing. But it does have to do with what I'm gonna tell ya. I treasure your friendship and hope that you feel the same, so I'm gonna tell you something that I'll ask you to swear on our friendship that you won't tell anyone else, at least not yet."

"You got it," was Jess' simple reply.

"Kylie just told me that she won't be in school for several days."

"So, she'll miss our last game?" interrupted Jess.

"She will." Timmy looked bewildered and at a loss for words before he continued, "I discovered recently that Kylie is a boy. It's probably about to become public, so now, more than ever, Kylie is gonna need some friends."

Timmy then gave Jess the Cliff Notes version of his discovery, his dad's relay of the information to Mrs. Pilsner, and his recent talk with Kylie. His story took most of their walk home, and when they reached their parting point, he assured her that he would let her know if and when he heard any more.

Psalm 25:5

"…guide me in your truth
and teach me, for You are
God, my Savior, and my
hope is in You all day long."

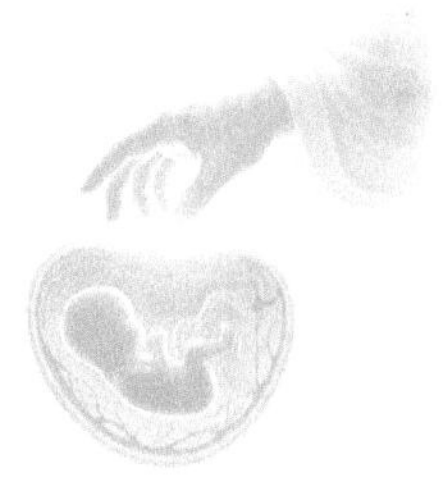

Chapter Eight

The next few days seemed to just fly by. In addition to his usual chores at home, the work he did for Gram around her house, and his schoolwork, Timmy sat several times with his mom and dad and once with Gram to discuss and seek advice about the widespread push for transgenderism. Surprisingly, what he thought would spread through the school like wildfire seemed to never even ignite a spark of interest. Jess told him that the team had been informed that Kylie was 'sick' and would be out of school for several days.

Timmy spoke with Pastor Remy and told him what little he knew about Kylie Winslow. He told the pastor about his brief conversation with Kylie and that, although she had started taking female hormones, it was his opinion that she was unconvinced about the entire transgender process and would be most willing to sit with the pastor should he agree to do so. Pastor Remy, of course, agreed. With Timmy as a go-between, they set a meeting for the second Monday in October, which was the Columbus holiday, a day off on the school calendar.

Aware that both Mom and Dad had busy lives and looked forward to the long weekend as an opportunity to get caught up on things around the house, Timmy imposed on Gram (who hardly ever said "no" to him) to take him to meet Kylie at the donut shop and bring them both to the 10:00 AM appointment with Pastor Remy. She willingly agreed to wait fifteen minutes or so outside the parsonage while Timmy went in with Kylie and made the necessary introductions. Pastor Remy, a sports fan who was very active with the youth of the church, chided Timmy for being lazy and not putting his athletic talents to use by playing a fall sport. His easygoing demeanor immediately put Kylie at ease and less on edge about their meeting.

After a few minutes, Timmy said, "Well, I'd better not keep Gram waiting, so I'll leave you guys to it." With that, he said his goodbyes and left. Pastor and Kylie didn't go into his office; instead, they sat comfortably in the living room. At about that time, Mrs. Remy entered the room with their three-year-old son in tow. Introductions were made, and their son, Jeremy, immediately sat next to Kylie.

"Oh, no, you don't," said Mrs. Remy, "We've got some shopping to do. Let's go."

After they left the room, the pastor broke the silence. "So, let's start at the beginning. Would you prefer I call you Kylie or Kyle?"

"I'm not sure" was the response.

"Well, how about Ky? It fits either way."

Kylie smiled, and you could almost see the anxiety drain away. For the next two hours, they talked as if they were old friends. For his part, Pastor Remy shared some of his past, especially the well-known story of how he had been so shy as a boy that he once got suspended from school because he adamantly refused to do a public speaking assignment. He confided that a "grandma-type" neighbor with the patience and understanding of a saint not only helped him overcome his shyness but was also instrumental in his calling to the ministry. "Imagine me, afraid of my own shadow, now standing before a church and giving sermons each week! Amazing what God can do."

The pastor made it easy for Kylie to speak about her past. She shared the bitter memories of having been lost and forgotten while living with her mom and dad's tumultuous relationship. Her home was in constant turmoil, and although specific memories were long ago buried away, unhappiness predominated their recall. The happy times were clearer, when Nana would rescue her from the grasp of her mom's alcohol addiction. Nana would tell her constantly how much she was cherished and loved; she took Kylie on exciting and memorable adventures. It was during those wonderful visits that Nana would have her wear a dress that she was "sewing for the underprivileged families of Appalachia."

Pastor learned that when Kylie's dad committed suicide and her mom was admitted to an alcohol recovery facility, Nana was awarded temporary custody. Kylie welcomed this, quickly dismissing the unhappy life with her mom and dad and embracing Nana's love and protection. Kylie could not remember how and when the "occasional" trying on of a dress became the normal day's outfit. Nana had always referred to Kylie as her "precious Kylie," and so Kylie seamlessly became her official name.

The two-hour interview flew by, and it was shortly after noon that Mrs. Remy returned. Pastor arose from his chair and helped his wife unload the groceries from the car. Without hesitation, Kylie jumped in and helped. When they were done, Mrs. Remy asked, "Kylie, I know that Timmy's Gram drove you here; what arrangements did you make for your return home?"

"Uh, we never got to that," responded Kylie.

"Well, how about you let me and Jeremy take you for a quick lunch and then home?"

Overwhelmed by the offer, Kylie could only respond with "Wow, you guys are so kind."

Pastor jumped in. "Before you leave, let me say that I have thoroughly enjoyed our visit. I don't know if I've helped you or not, but should you be so inclined, our church, The Way, is affiliated with a group of Christian counselors who are way more trained to help people with life's crises. If you would like, I'd be happy to arrange a meeting." With that, he reached over to the small table next to the couch and grabbed a pocket bible. "Perhaps when you get the chance, you can look this over. Whatever your questions, the answers are here."

With that, Mrs. Remy, Jeremy, and Kylie left the parsonage and headed to the local sandwich shop for a quick lunch. Kylie was very much at ease, speaking with the pastor's wife as though they were long-lost friends. After lunch, Mrs. Remy drove the short distance to the Bartram home. As Kylie grabbed her things and prepared to say goodbye, Mrs. Remy reached over and gave her a big hug. "Kylie, I'm not much on giving advice, especially when it hasn't been asked for, but I know a life-altering crisis when I see one. I can't claim to understand the issues that have brought you to this point and the decisions that you now face. I am deeply saddened by the 'answers' that have been popularized by an atheistic worldview. While transgenderism has been around for centuries, it's only been popularized in recent times; you may not know that it is a huge money maker for some surgeons, hospitals, and Big Pharma. Mutilation of the precious creation that God has made in you is not the answer, and all too many who have chosen that path are now finding that those irreversible choices, foisted upon them by an unknowing world, have proven harmful. Recent studies have shown that compared to cisgender adults, transgender adults were seven times more likely to contemplate suicide, four times more likely to attempt it, and eight times more likely to engage in non-suicidal self-injury. I could go on and on, but my point is to urge you to be cautious and thorough in your decision-making. I am absolutely biased, but seeking wisdom from your Maker is where you should begin. That Bible that my husband gave you has the answers that you're looking for. Start with the opening pages of the first book, the book of Genesis. Read carefully Chapter 1, verse 27. Clearly, God created male and female. He didn't create 'in-betweens.' He didn't create options to change one's sex. In fact, even science tells us that, aberrations excepted, people are born with XX or XY chromosomes. No hormone therapy or surgery can change your chromosome configuration."

Kylie listened intently. What Mrs. Remy was suggesting was certainly not what she had been told by the counselors and physicians who had urged her to make the transition from male to female. So many questions were running through her mind; yet, she knew that now was neither the time nor the place to ask them. She was grateful for the lunch and the ride home, but also sensitive to Mrs. Remy's schedule and reluctant to take more of her time. "Mrs. Remy, thank you so much for everything; I appreciate your generosity of lunch and the ride home, but more than that, I am grateful for the love that you and Pastor have extended. I hope to see you and Jeremy again." She reached over and grabbed Jeremy's hand to shake hands, but he had other ideas. He jumped up on her lap and gave her a big hug. "Bye, Jeremy," was all she could get out.

As Kylie disembarked from the car, Mrs. Remy leaned over and said, "Don't forget Pastor's offer for the Christian counseling. And, most of all, remember this: God doesn't make mistakes."

Later that evening, Kylie called Timmy and told him about her meetings with Pastor and Mrs. Remy. She thanked him for making the contact, told him that she would be making the connection with the Christian counseling group, and hinted that she probably wouldn't return to school for a while.

Acts 3:16

"By faith in the name of Jesus, this man whom you see and know was made strong. It is Jesus' name and the faith that comes through Him that has given this complete healing to him, as you can all see."

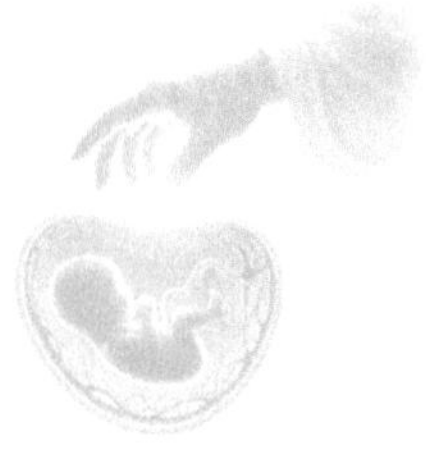

Chapter Nine

In the weeks that followed, life for Timmy resumed its normal pace. Kylie wasn't present in school and remained on homebound tutoring. The only exception was Awards Night, because Mrs. Pilsner had called her and asked that she be there. A few of her classmates and teammates inquired about her whereabouts, but since she hadn't been especially outgoing and friendly, she was soon "out of sight, out of mind." Timmy and Jess both phoned her on separate occasions, and one Saturday, they paid her a visit.

"I am so glad to see you guys," she exclaimed. "Can't tell you how excited I was when Jess texted me that you might come over today. All I seem to do is schoolwork and counseling sessions, so this visit is a great break."

"Yeah, well, school's no bed of roses either,"

Timmy piped in, adding, "I told you we'd do whatever we could to help, so if a simple visit helps, I'm up for it."

"Ditto," said Jess. "How are you doing with the counseling?"

"The counseling sessions are hard, but good, if that makes any sense. I see a guy by the name of Mr. Bell, who is very caring, and who has been leading me through resurrecting memories that I had long ago buried in the memory graveyard."

Jess pulled out a paper bag and handed it to Kylie. "Thought you could use a little gift, maybe give you something to do besides homework. You do know that 'all work and no play makes Kylie a dull person.' If you wanna open it now, you, Timmy, and me can give it a test drive around the track."

Kylie opened the bag and pulled out the game Jenga. Her smile seemed to stretch from one ear to the other. For the next couple of hours, the three of them howled and laughed as they went from one crashed tower to another.

Finally, Jess said, "I hate to interrupt this Jenga balancing act, but I've gotta get going." Turning to Kylie, she said, "I know you liked your meeting with Pastor Remy. I attend the Catholic Church in my old town, but if you'd like to go to The Way some Sunday for Service, I'd be happy to meet up with you and go. I've been there several times with Timmy.

Pastor always gives a great sermon."

Walking Timmy and Jess to the door, Kylie ushered them on their way, saying, "Thanks so much, you guys, for the visit. Can't begin to tell you what it means to me. Sometimes just having company is the best help."

A few Sundays after Columbus Day weekend, Timmy, Mom, Dad, and Gram were talking with some friends after the church service when Timmy looked up and saw Jess and Kylie. On this particular Sunday, Jess and Kylie sat toward the rear of the church, and Timmy didn't even know that they were there until he saw them at coffee hour.

Kylie looked good; there was an air of ease or comfort about her. Timmy didn't quite know how to read it, but he did notice that the French braid was gone and that Kylie was now wearing her hair in a pixie-style cut. After they said their hellos, Kylie indicated that she was going to hunt down Pastor Remy and tell him about her counseling sessions with the dysphoria specialist, Mr. Bell, from the Christian counseling group that Pastor Remy had recommended. After Kylie left, Jess began a brief discussion with Timmy. "I was kinda shocked"—she began—"when Kylie called and asked me to keep her company and come here to church this Sunday. I wasn't too sure last Saturday about asking her; now I'm so glad I did."

"Well, I gotta say," responded Timmy, "you're not as shocked as I was to see the two of you." He paused before continuing. "As a matter of fact, I'm shocked by all the happenings of the past few weeks. Heck, I might have been aware of things like gender dysphoria, but knowing Kylie and being even a small part of her struggle has really been an eye-opener. I'm finding out that I've actually led a pretty sheltered life. This morning, when Pastor Remy talked about hope, it got me to wondering, *'How do people handle this stuff without faith and trust in God?'*"

Jess responded with, "I loved his ending when he spoke of God's overwhelming love and then personalized that love by quoting Jeremiah 29:11, 'For I know the plans I have for you, declared the Lord, plans to prosper you and not harm you, plans to give you hope and a future.'"

"Reminds me of something he told our confirmation class last year when he quoted some guy—I forgot who—'God loves you so much that if He had a refrigerator, your picture would be on it.'"

"Hey, I like that," said Jess. "Gotta remember to pass that one along to Kylie."

Later that night, Timmy sat with his mom and dad before heading off to bed. He told them about Kylie having met with Pastor Remy and about Mrs. Remy having taken Kylie for lunch before bringing her home. He also said that Kylie had told him and

Jess that she would remain on homebound tutoring for an indefinite period, continue living with the Bartrams, who were supporting her, and attend counseling sessions with the Christian counseling group.

Dad, in turn, related what was happening on the school front. "If you haven't already heard," he began, "Mr. Hogan has been removed from his position as Athletic Director. Apparently, since he willingly allowed Kylie to play on the girls' soccer team and thus violated the rules of the Interscholastic Committee, both the superintendent and the principal were obligated to remove him from that position. He will continue as a PE teacher for Wynhope High.

"There is some question as to what Coach Bennett knew and when he might have known it, so there will be no action taken against him. Regardless, he has resigned his position as coach. Unfortunately for the team, the seven wins on the season will be forfeited and the official team record for the season will go in the books as 0 - 11."

"As I understand it," injected Mom, "the Bartrams have agreed to become Kylie's temporary guardians for as long as she remains in Wynhope. Of course, that is dependent on the approval of Kylie, her ailing grandmother, and the courts. You know, it's not an accident that we're aware of Kylie's situation, and it's so important that we pray for her. But we also should pray for all those affected by sexual dysphoria and its impact on society."

"I don't follow ya," said Timmy.

Mom thought a moment before continuing. "Sex change is but one of a host of issues brought to the forefront by the sexual revolution of the 60s and 70s. Abortion, same sex marriage, and gay rights, to name but a few, have been around since the fall of man, but only fairly recently have become issues in our political agendas."

"Yeah, but God's on our side, right?" quipped Timmy.

"Sadly," Dad chimed in, "God doesn't choose sides. As the saying goes, 'It's not a matter of whose side God is on; it's a matter of who is on God's side.'"

Mom continued. "To my way of thinking, the lines of separation between morality and legality have become blurred, and so some things that are not in keeping with God's will have been embraced by segments of society and deemed legal in light of the law. To the point, Kylie may be on the verge of hormonal and surgical interventions that would mutilate the body and attempt to alter God's creation. This, we believe, is against God's law, yet it may very well be legal."

"Yeah, but didn't God put Kylie in the wrong body?" asked Timmy.

"Timmy, that's a lie straight from hell," answered

Dad. "God does not make mistakes! If He did, He wouldn't be God!"

"Let's just remember," reminded Mom, "as Christians, we are called to love those suffering from a variety of gender dysphorias as well as those who may promote solutions not in keeping with our beliefs. There are so many places in scripture where we're commanded to love each other, but none are as clear as the second of the two great commandments that Jesus taught in Matthew 22:39, where He says, '…Love your neighbor as yourself.' There are times when we might not agree with a person's choices, but that should never stop us from loving them."

With the discussion winding down and the hour getting late, Mom said, "Before you go off to bed, young man, I think we should spend a few moments in prayer and share our thoughts and concerns with our Savior. Remember, Matthew 18:20 says, 'For where two or three come together in my name, there am I with them.'"

They fell to their knees and thanked God for His presence and for having heard their previous comments. They thanked Him that already He had orchestrated Kylie's meeting with the Remys and that she seemed at ease counseling with Mr. Bell. They asked for wisdom for so many struggling with gender issues and ended by asking God to enable them to always show love to those in need. When they finished, Timmy thanked Mom & Dad for their wise words, gave them both a big hug, and started to leave. Mom called out after him, “Have a peaceful rest.”

Timmy turned and responded, “How could I not? We just prayed as a team, and we did it with our ‘Most Valuable Teammate’ praying with us.”

Psalm 34:7

“The angel of the Lord encamps around those who fear Him, and He delivers them.”

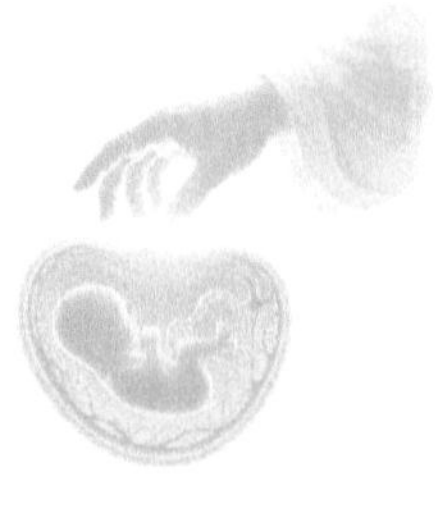

Epilogue

Six Months Later

"Timothy Albert Dennison, what on earth is the matter with you? You're pacing around like a caged lion. If I didn't know better, I'd think you'd been out rolling around in a poison ivy patch."

"You know what today is, right, Mom?"

"How could I not know? You've been crowin' about it for the past week."

"Well, opening day, first home game is a big thing."

"You should be so excited about one of your algebra tests!"

"Oh, c'mon; will ya stop with the algebra stuff?" Quick to change the subject, Timmy said, "You guys are coming to the game today, right? You and Dad promised. Oh, and I told Gram that you guys would pick her up, so don't forget."

"Aye, aye, sir!" said Mom as she saluted in mock obedience.

It had been a long winter. The snowfall had been heavier and more frequent than normal. Between his house and Gram's house, Timmy felt as though he'd shoveled enough snow to fill Fenway Park. On the upside, he'd grown an inch or two and put on a good twenty or so pounds of muscle. He'd gone into spring tryouts for Wynhope Baseball with the confidence of a "lean, mean fighting machine." Wynhope had graduated several baseball veterans the previous June. Because of that, they faced a tough, potentially losing season (or as Dad called it, "a character-building season"). The good thing about that was the opportunity, and Timmy was rewarded for being one of two freshmen who would be in the starting lineup.

As he grabbed his book bag and his equipment bag and headed for the door, he once more reminded Mom, "Game starts at 3:30, and don't forget to pick up Gram."

"Good luck," called Mom as he slammed the door and headed out to meet up with Jess for the walk to school.

"You got the heebie-jeebies?" was Jess' greeting when she arrived at their meeting spot and saw him already there and pacing.

"Yeah, well, you will, too, next week when the softball season opens."

As they walked and talked, Timmy seemed to settle a bit as Jess reminded him of some of the pointers she had given him on hitting. Jess could hit from both sides of the plate and had set literally every record in the Wynhope Little League books. Although she was a natural, she was never content; she read and studied everything she could get her hands on that would improve her understanding of the hitting techniques. Throughout the winter, she and Timmy had worked on hand positioning, bat weight and length, and a variety of hand-eye coordination drills. As they approached the school, she said, "OK, I won't see ya 'til after the game. I'd wish ya good luck, but you don't need it. You got this. Piece of cake." With that, they parted.

The day in school seemed to drag by. During his lunch shift, Timmy sat with the other team members who had the same lunch shift. The upperclassmen recalled their two losses to the Monarchs the previous season and were especially anxious about facing their star pitcher in the day's game. Finally, the end-of-the-day bell rang, and Timmy all but ran to the locker room to dress for the game. Once in uniform and out on the field, the business of baseball and playing to his best took over.

Meanwhile, Mom's day probably wouldn't go down as one of her best. Gram called around 10:00 to remind her that she had promised to drive Gram to her doctor's appointment at 11:00. Totally distracted by coordinating everything for Timmy's game, Mom had completely forgotten about the appointment. She dropped what she was doing, quickly changed, and rushed down the street to get Gram, who came running out as soon as Mom pulled into her driveway. They got to the doctor's office twenty minutes later, only to be told by the receptionist that the doctor had had an emergency and wouldn't be able to see Gram until 2:30. Even if the doctor were on time (and doctors seldom are), they would hardly have time to make it for Timmy's game at 3:30. They were about to cancel when, miraculously, a cancellation came in and the 2:00 slot opened up. Even though that would still be tight, they booked it. Rather than rush home and then rush back, they decided to go for a leisurely lunch. Mom knew that even if the game started on time and only went seven innings, they wouldn't be having dinner until later than usual.

Mom and Gram had a casual lunch and got to spend some precious time together, something they hadn't been able to do for quite some time. The doctor was on time (wow, that's a first), but the half hour they gained by taking the 2:00 appointment was lost in the time it took to go for the blood test that the doctor had ordered. "We can still make it," said Gram as they hurried from the lab to the car.

"I highly doubt it," sighed Mom as she stared at

a flat front tire. "Can this day get any worse? Timmy is gonna be so disappointed."

As only God could orchestrate, a young boy, not much older than Timmy, came out of the lab, saw their problem, and within minutes, he expertly changed the tire. When Mom tried to slip him a few bucks, he simply said, "Just pay it forward, Ma'am," and disappeared before they could object.

"Did we just meet an angel?" asked Gram.

"Maybe. The way the day has gone so far, it's sure looking like God keeps clearing the way for us to get to Timmy's game."

When they finally met up with Dad at the high school parking lot, he was just dialing his phone to find out where they were. "Hurry up," he shouted. "We've already missed the warm-ups and probably some of the game."

Hurriedly, Mom relayed the events of the day, ending with, "You're lucky we're here at all. Thank the good Lord for His watchful angels."

"So," replied Dad, "kinda reminds me of the *Footprints in the Sand* poem. When you look back on the day, can you see the single set of footprints, those troubling parts of the day when God was carrying you?"

Hoping that Timmy hadn't noticed their absence, they grabbed their lawn chairs and hustled to the hillside where they would have a good view of the field. Just as they were negotiating their spots, the opposing pitcher finished his warm-up pitches, and the catcher made his throw to second base. The announcer grabbed his mic and announced, "Leading off the bottom of the second inning for the Wynhope Wildcats, and batting in the number six spot, is their freshman right fielder … Kyle Winslow."

Dad turned to Mom and Gram, smiled, and proclaimed, "Yup. Kinda looks like the Lord's been doing more heavy carrying than we could have imagined!"

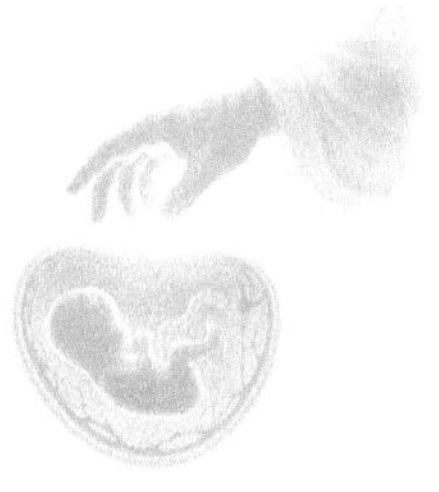

Acknowledgments

I am blessed to have been raised by loving parents who were my first teachers, mentors, and spiritual examples. In addition to the foundational training of my parents, I'm grateful for the spiritual background fostered by the priests and brothers of Holy Family Monastery in Farmington, CT, for whom I worked as a pre-teen. Throughout the years I have known many clergy from a variety of spiritual disciplines, all of whom have enriched my theological values. I am also blessed with a loving and talented family at Bakerville Church, a member of the newly formed Global Methodist Church.

I'm indebted to my wife, Marlene and granddaughter, Barrie for their wisdom in suggesting significant changes to a draft that could easily have been too rich in preaching and politics, and not rich enough in love and understanding. Such a balance is most difficult in merging the hard words of a caring and loving God with everyday Christian living.

I am most appreciative that there is a venue like Dove Christian Publishers and Inscript Publishing where God's truth is celebrated. Thanks, Allison, for your insight and help.

Of course, it goes without saying, that only an Almighty God could design and orchestrate all the ideas, concepts, and nuances that meld theological truth with simple storytelling. Amen.

www.ingramcontent.com/pod-product-compliance
Lightning Source LLC
Chambersburg PA
CBHW020524310726
48979CB00014B/2201/J
* 9 7 8 1 9 5 7 4 9 7 6 6 2 *